MR. QUIET

by Roger Hargreaves

Mr Quiet liked the quiet life.

He lived, quietly, in a small little cottage in the middle of a wood.

The problem was, that small little cottage was in the middle of a wood in the middle of a country called Loudland!

Everything and everybody in Loudland was noisy.

Oh, the noise!

Dogs didn't go "woof" like dogs you know.

They went (take a deep breath) "WOOF!"

People didn't shut their doors like you or I would shut our doors.

They slammed them.

BANG!

People didn't talk to each other.

They shouted at each other.

"HELLO," they'd shout as they met in the street.

And, you've heard about something being as quiet as a mouse, haven't you?

Not in Loudland.

They had the noisiest mice in the world.

"SQUEAK! SQUEAK!" they'd roar at each other.

Mr Noisy would have liked living in Loudland.

He'd have loved it.

But Mr Quiet didn't.

Noise frightened him.

So, he stayed in his cottage in the middle of his wood as much as he could.

But of course he couldn't stay there all the time.

Every week, for instance, he had to go shopping.

He used to creep into the grocer's shop.

"GOOD MORNING," bellowed the grocer.
"WHAT CAN I DO FOR YOU?"

"Please," whispered Mr Quiet, "could I have some cornflakes please?"

"WHAT?"

"Cornflakes. Please," he whispered.

"SPEAK UP!"

Mr Quiet tried his loudest whisper.

"Cornflakes."

"CAN'T HEAR YOU," shouted the grocer. "NEXT PLEASE!"

And poor Mr Quiet had to creep away without any cornflakes.

It wasn't fair, was it?

He crept into the butcher's.

"Please," he whispered, "I'd like some meat."

The butcher didn't even hear him.

He was humming to himself, loudly and fiercely.

Mr Quiet tried again.

"Please," he whispered, "I'd like some meat."

The butcher started to whistle.

It sounded more like a burglar alarm than a whistle.

Mr Quiet fled.

Empty handed.

It often happened, which probably explains why he was so little.

Poor Mr Quiet.

He sat at home that night with a feeling of despair.

"Whatever am I to do?" he thought.

"It's no use," he thought, "I'll just have to try again."

And so, the following day, he went shopping again.

But, the same thing happened.

"CAN'T HEAR YOU," thundered the grocer. "NEXT PLEASE!"

"CAN'T HEAR YOU," bellowed the greengrocer. "NEXT PLEASE!"

"CAN'T HEAR YOU," roared the milkman. "NEXT PLEASE!"

"CAN'T HEAR YOU," boomed the butcher. "NEXT PLEASE!"

Oh dear!

Poor Mr Quiet went home and went to bed.

Hungry.

The morning after he was awakened by a noise which sounded like bombs dropping.

It was the Loudland postman knocking at Mr Quiet's door.

BANG! BANG! BANG! BANG!

Mr Quiet went and opened the door.

"MORNING," shouted the postman. "LETTER FOR YOU!"

Mr Quiet took the letter into his kitchen.

He sat down to open it.

He waited until the noise of the postman's footsteps died away.

CLUMP CLUMP CLUMP CLUMP clump clump.

Mr Quiet opened the letter in great excitement.

He'd never had a letter before.

It was from Mr Happy in Happyland.

An invitation!

To stay!

Mr Quiet was overjoyed.

He rushed upstairs and packed his bag and set off that very morning.

It was late when he arrived on Mr Happy's doorstep.

He knocked on Mr Happy's door.

Tap tap tap.

Mr Happy opened the door.

"Hello," he smiled. "I thought I heard something. You must be Mr Quiet. Well, don't just stand there, come in and have some supper."

It was the first proper meal Mr Quiet had had for months. And while he was eating it he told Mr Happy all about the problems he'd been having in Loudland.

Mr Happy was most sympathetic.

Over breakfast the following morning, Mr Happy told Mr Quiet that he'd been thinking about his problem.

"I think," he said, "that under the circumstances you'd better stay here in Happyland."

Mr Quiet's face lit up.

"And," continued Mr Happy, "we'll find you a house, and," he went on, "a job."

Mr Quiet's face dropped.

"I'm not very good at jobs," he confessed, "because I'm too quiet."

"Ah," smiled Mr Happy. "I have the very job for a quiet chap like you!"

And so, the very next day, Mr Quiet started work.

And he loves it.

Do you know where he works?

In the Happy Lending Library!

As you know, everybody who goes into a library has to be very quiet, and only whispering is allowed.

What a clever idea of Mr Happy's, wasn't it?

And these days, Mr Quiet is as happy as can be.

Why, only the other day, do you know what he did on his way home from work?

He was so happy he laughed out loud.

Can you imagine?

Tee hee hee!

"NEXT PLEASE!"

3 Great Offers for MR. MEN Fans!

MR. MEN TOKEN

1 New Mr. Men or Little Miss Library Bus Presentation Cases

A brand new stronger, roomier school bus library box, with sturdy carrying handle and stay-closed fasteners.
The full colour, wipe-clean boxes make a great home for your full collection.
They're just £5.99 inc P&P and free bookmark!

☐ MR. MEN   ☐ LITTLE MISS (please tick and order overleaf)

PLEASE STICK YOUR 50P COIN HERE

2 Door Hangers and Posters

In every Mr. Men and Little Miss book like this one, you will find a special token. Collect 6 tokens and we will send you a brilliant Mr. Men or Little Miss poster and a Mr. Men or Little Miss double sided full colour bedroom door hanger of your choice. Simply tick your choice in the list and tape a 50p coin for your two items to this page.

Door Hangers (please tick)
☐ Mr. Nosey & Mr. Muddle
☐ Mr. Slow & Mr. Busy
☐ Mr. Messy & Mr. Quiet
☐ Mr. Perfect & Mr. Forgetful
☐ Little Miss Fun & Little Miss Late
☐ Little Miss Helpful & Little Miss Tidy
☐ Little Miss Busy & Little Miss Brainy
☐ Little Miss Star & Little Miss Fun

Posters (please tick)
☐ MR.MEN
☐ LITTLE MISS

3 **Sixteen Beautiful Fridge Magnets –** any **2** for **£2.00!** inc.P&P

They're very special collector's items!
Simply tick your first and second* choices from the list below
of any 2 characters!

1st Choice

- ☐ Mr. Happy
- ☐ Mr. Lazy
- ☐ Mr. Topsy-Turvy
- ☐ Mr. Bounce
- ☐ Mr. Bump
- ☐ Mr. Small
- ☐ Mr. Snow
- ☐ Mr. Wrong

- ☐ Mr. Daydream
- ☐ Mr. Tickle
- ☐ Mr. Greedy
- ☐ Mr. Funny
- ☐ Little Miss Giggles
- ☐ Little Miss Splendid
- ☐ Little Miss Naughty
- ☐ Little Miss Sunshine

2nd Choice

- ☐ Mr. Happy
- ☐ Mr. Lazy
- ☐ Mr. Topsy-Turvy
- ☐ Mr. Bounce
- ☐ Mr. Bump
- ☐ Mr. Small
- ☐ Mr. Snow
- ☐ Mr. Wrong

- ☐ Mr. Daydream
- ☐ Mr. Tickle
- ☐ Mr. Greedy
- ☐ Mr. Funny
- ☐ Little Miss Giggles
- ☐ Little Miss Splendid
- ☐ Little Miss Naughty
- ☐ Little Miss Sunshine

*Only in case your first choice is out of stock.

TO BE COMPLETED BY AN ADULT

**To apply for any of these great offers, ask an adult to complete the coupon below and send it with
the appropriate payment and tokens, if needed, to MR. MEN OFFERS, PO BOX 7, MANCHESTER M19 2HD**

☐ Please send _____ Mr. Men Library case(s) and/or _____ Little Miss Library case(s) at £5.99 each inc P&P

☐ Please send a poster and door hanger as selected overleaf. I enclose six tokens plus a 50p coin for P&P

☐ Please send me _____ pair(s) of Mr. Men/Little Miss fridge magnets, as selected above at £2.00 inc P&P

Fan's Name _____

Address _____

_____ **Postcode** _____

Date of Birth _____

Name of Parent/Guardian _____

Total amount enclosed £ _____

☐ **I enclose a cheque/postal order payable to Egmont Books Limited**

☐ **Please charge my MasterCard/Visa/Amex/Switch or Delta account** (delete as appropriate)

Card Number

Expiry date ___/___ **Signature** _____

Please allow 28 days for delivery. Offer is only available while stocks last. We reserve the right to change the terms
of this offer at any time and we offer a 14 day money back guarantee. This does not affect your statutory rights.
Data Protection Act: If you do not wish to receive other similar offers from us or companies we recommend, please
tick this box ☐. Offers apply to UK only.

MR. MEN **LITTLE MISS**
Mr. Men and Little Miss™ & ©Mrs. Roger Hargreaves

CUT ALONG DOTTED LINE AND RETURN THIS WHOLE PAGE